Adapted by Alice Alfonsi

Based on the television series, "Phil of the Future", created by Douglas Tuber & Tim Maile

Part One is based on the episode written by Douglas Tuber & Tim Maile

Part Two is based on the episode written by Tom Burkhard & Matt Dearborn

New York

Copyright © 2005 Disney Enterprises, Inc.

All rights reserved. No part of this book may be reproduced
or transmitted in any form or by any means, electronic or
mechanical, including photocopying, recording, or by any
information storage and retrieval system, without written
permission from the publisher.
For information address
Disney Press, 114 Fifth Avenue,
New York, New York 10011-5690.

Printed in the United States of America

First Edition
1 3 5 7 9 10 8 6 4 2

Library of Congress Control Number: 2005922042

ISBN 0-7868-3846-9

For more Disney Press fun, visit www.disneybooks.com
Visit DisneyChannel.com

If you purchased this book without a cover, you should be aware
that this book is stolen property. It was reported as "unsold and
destroyed" to the publisher, and neither the author nor the
publisher has received any payment for this "stripped" book.

PART ONE

CHAPTER ONE

For Phil Diffy, living in the past had its advantages. First of all, antigravity cells hadn't been invented yet. So his recreational air vehicle pretty much had the run of the rooftops in his town.

Secondly, his education took place in a *real* school instead of a virtual one. So he was able to make a friend like Keely Teslow, the coolest and nicest girl in *any* century.

And, finally, he could predict what was going to happen in the future—because he was *from* the future. Of course, Phil could only predict the big-picture stuff, like Unification Day and the biological end of the human little toe. For the trivial stuff, like what his little sister, Pim, was going to do to try to wreck his life, he was pretty much on his own.

At least he'd won the most recent battle in their sibling war. After dinner, their dad had thrown a glowing Skyak orb into the air. Phil had caught it before Pim. So, of course, she was furious. Gadgets from the future like the Skyak were as scarce in this time period as Cheeseola, Phil's favorite cheese-flavored sparkling soda.

Most of the time, Mr. Diffy kept their toys from the future locked up. He said they couldn't be too careful. If their neighbors found out their RV was really a broken-down Fleet Flyer 6000 time-travel machine, the government would probably lock the Diffys up in a lab for the rest of their lives. *Not* a good ending to their time-travel vacation, Phil figured.

As he strode across the back porch with a

triumphant grin, Phil tossed the pulsing Skyak orb from one hand to the other. Pim stomped onto the porch right behind him. Her sneakers actually made the floorboards shudder. But Phil wasn't intimidated.

"Pim," he warned, "*I'm* using it first."

Pim folded her arms and glared. "Why?"

"Because," he replied. "I'm older—"

Pim lunged for the orb. Phil jerked it away.

"I'm smarter," he added.

She lunged again. He lifted it high.

"And *taller*," he finished.

"Phil, you may be taller," Pim replied, "but there's always going to be one thing that I have over you."

"Yeah. What's that?" he asked. "A serious *anger* issue?"

Pim shook her long, blond pigtails. "I can hold a grudge *forever*," she declared.

Phil rolled his eyes. "Oh, really?"

"Yes," said Pim. "Remember the time you ate the last butterscotch-pudding cup?"

"No," answered Phil.

"Well, you did," snapped Pim. "I was four and a half. It was Tuesday. Six-thirty-five. You were wearing blue."

Phil shook his head and tossed the orb onto the backyard lawn. *Sheesh*, he thought, only my disturbed little sister would turn a missing pudding cup into the crime of the twenty-second century.

On the grass, the glowing orb began to blink. With a blinding flash, it transformed into what looked like a purple snowmobile. Instead of runners, however, it sported antigravity cells. Phil climbed onto the vehicle's seat and pulled on his helmet.

"Pim, I didn't eat your pudding cup," he assured her as he gripped the handles of the Skyak and revved its engine. "I put it in your shampoo!"

Before Pim could launch herself at her brother, Phil launched himself into the night air. "Yee-hah!" he cried. Then he gleefully escaped his sister's fury in a dazzling cloud of Skyak dust.

Pim's foul mood followed her all the way to school the next day. H.G. Wells Junior/Senior High was a primitive sort of institution, in Pim's opinion. Children sat at desks placed in neat little rows and listened to *live* teachers for six or more hours a day.

It was nothing like the virtual classes Pim had attended in 2121. In the future, she'd simply sit in a Comfa-cliner, place her Virtu-teacher visor over her eyes, and let the day's lesson play before her like a 3-D movie.

Pim didn't share her brother's enthusiasm for the past. Here in this stupid time period, she grumbled to herself, I have to put up with ancient technology. Plus I'm forced to interact with annoyingly simple minds—like the one in the hall up ahead.

"Berwick," Pim growled, walking up to her goody-goody classmate.

Debbie Berwick was wearing one of her typical preppy outfits—a plaid skirt, string of pearls, and spotless patterned sweater with matching headband.

Yuck, thought Pim, even Sally Sunshine's *clothes* annoy me! Pim preferred the rebel look. Today she wore a denim skirt, funky brown-and-white-striped tights, and a long-sleeved T-shirt displaying the words PUNK 08.

"Let me guess what's going on here," said Pim, looking over the items in Debbie's hands. "Hot coffee, sports section, standing outside Mr. Hackett's office . . . you're either a) loopy, b) the world's biggest kiss-up, or c) a combo platter."

"Pim, I do this for all my teachers," Debbie explained with a big, happy grin. "In fact, would you like to run up a pastry to Ms. Selletti's office?"

Help a teacher? thought Pim. "Uh, no."

Just then, Mr. Hackett's voice came through his office door. "I know it's expensive," he was saying, "but I have to have the operation."

Curious, Pim tiptoed to the door and pushed it open slightly. She leaned her ear up to the opening.

Debbie's smile instantly disappeared. "Eavesdropping is wrong for seven reasons," she primly announced to Pim. "And I'll explain why. First of all—"

"Debbie, *shush!*" whispered Pim. She peeked into the office.

Mr. Hackett continued his phone conversation. "Well, if I don't have the operation," he went on, shaking his bald head, "my life will be worthless. Just a big zilch-o."

Debbie's eyes widened in alarm. "Ohmigosh, Pim," she whispered, pulling her classmate away from the door. "Mr. Hackett is sick and needs an operation. You know what this calls for? A fund-raiser!" Debbie clapped her hands with glee.

"Oh, whoa, whoa, whoa," said Pim, throwing up her hands. "Every time someone needs help, you're all, '*I'll help you.*' And I'm all, '*Get over it.'* And you're all, *'To the fund-raising mobile!'*"

"Pim, that's okay," said Debbie, her voice full of pity. "Fund-raising isn't for everybody."

As Debbie walked away, Pim narrowed her eyes and snarled, "What is she saying? That *I* can't fund-raise? Well, it's on, Berwick!"

"What's on?" asked Debbie, suddenly reappearing at Pim's side.

"Stop that!" cried Pim, shuddering. If there's one thing Berwick and her batlike hearing can do, thought Pim, it's freak me out!

Meanwhile, inside his office, Mr. Hackett continued to discuss his operation with Maurice, the man on the other end of the phone line. "The only procedure I can afford is the one-zero-six," Mr. Hackett admitted. He picked up the *I Can't Believe It's a Toupee!* brochure on his desk and took a closer look at the "before" and "after" pictures.

"Yeah, that's not a hair-replacement system," Mr. Hackett complained, "that's a toilet seat cover parted down the middle."

On the other end of the line, Maurice suggested Mr. Hackett consider another option—like wearing a cap to cover his baldness. But Mr. Hackett declared, "No, no, no. I want it." The teacher took one more look at the brochure—and the tall, blond women smiling at the man in the "after" picture.

"Okay, I *will* still attract big Norwegian women like the guy on the cover, right?" Mr. Hackett asked.

Maurice told the teacher he was sure to get twice as much attention as the man in the brochure.

"Oh, Maurice," Mr. Hackett replied, "you hound dog!"

CHAPTER TWO

"**P**hil, you know what this is?" Keely asked at the start of lunch period. She stood in front of him, holding up a long, silver tube.

Phil tensed like a contestant on a TV game show. His best friend in this century had just quizzed him on a twenty-first-century artifact.

Okay, he thought, scratching his head. I didn't spend hours studying history for nothing. I *know* it's a primitive musical instrument. Woodwind family. *Think, think. . . .*

"It's a flute!" Phil blurted out.

"No," said Keely.

Phil's jaw dropped. He couldn't believe he'd guessed wrong.

"It's a musical spit catcher!" Keely declared with disgust. She'd just come from band practice, where she'd taken playing off-key to a whole new level. With a sigh, she released the flute's spit valve. A river of unnecessary saliva trickled down the silver tube.

Phil cringed. "Nice," he said sarcastically. If that's not a *primitive* instrument, I don't know what is, he thought.

Keely shuddered. "Phil, that can't be healthy."

"Here." Phil handed her his unopened container of orange juice. "Rehydrate."

As Keely drank, Phil threw her a smile. She looks really pretty today, he thought. Keely was wearing black athletic pants and a bright pink jacket. A yellow knit cap hugged the top of her head, making the golden curls that spilled to her shoulders seem even more bouncy.

But Keely herself didn't seem very bouncy. Sighing, she plopped down in the seat across from him. "I don't know why I thought I could play the flute," she complained, looking defeated. "Did you ever play an instrument?"

"Yeah, a fybel," Phil replied without thinking.

Keely's brow wrinkled. She'd never heard of a fybel. "Did you blow in it?" she asked, stealing one of his french fries. "Are there strings? Did you hit it?"

Phil nervously looked down at his lunch tray. "Exactly, all those things."

He'd forgotten that fybels hadn't been invented yet. Neither had transboxes or boomatogs. *Wow*, he thought, when you come right down to it, this century's music has barely crawled out of the primal cave.

"So I tried to call you last night to talk about the field trip," said Keely.

"Oh." Phil knew why he'd missed the call. For hours last night, he'd been ripping up clouds on his Skyak. "Yeah, I was out riding my bike," he lied, nervously stuffing fries into his mouth.

Keely frowned. "Really? Your mom said you went for a walk."

Phil tensed. *Uh-oh*, he thought, better think of something fast. "Yeah, I did," he amended. "Well, see, I took a bike ride, but then I got a flat tire, so I had to walk the bike back. So, *technically*, I guess it was really a walk."

Keely looked a little suspicious. So Phil quickly changed the subject. "Anyway," he said, "about the field trip? Where are we going?"

"To the Pickford tomato ranch!" said Keely, finally brightening. "You didn't know Pickford was the ketchup capital of the world, did you?"

"That's why there's a giant squeeze bottle in the town square?" he guessed. All this talk of ketchup made him hungry for some. He reached for the huge plastic bottle sitting on the table and squeezed a fat ribbon of ketchup along his hot dog.

"I know it sounds lame," Keely admitted, "but it's actually kind of cool." She grinned, obviously excited about the trip. "At the end of the tour, everybody gets into the stomping tub and stomps tomatoes. Anyway, it's all squishy and messy and barefoot."

Phil's brown eyes widened in alarm. "Barefoot? As in *barefoot*?"

"Yeah. What's the matter?" Keely asked.

Phil frantically shook his head. "Oh, I can't."

Keely didn't understand. "Can't *what*?"

"Go to Pickford Ranch," Phil replied, "because, uh . . . I'm allergic to tomatoes. If one even touches my body, I get all weird and twitchy." He made his eyes blink crazily, then jerked his head to the side. "See? Just like that."

Keely pointed to the plate on his lunch tray. She could hardly even see the hot dog under all the ketchup he'd poured over it. "You're about to eat ketchup right now."

"I am? Oh!" Phil could think of no other way around this one. Pretending Keely had just done him a *huge* favor, he picked up the dog, bun and all, and tossed it over his shoulder.

Good riddance! Phil pretended to be thinking as he brushed one palm against the other. Then he heard a loud squawk. Turning, he saw that his flying, ketchup-covered hot dog had just clocked some poor dude in the head.

Ooooh, my bad, he thought.

For the rest of the school day, Phil tried to think of anything but the Pickford Ranch field trip. But his mind just wouldn't let it go. In geometry, his octagon morphed into a tomato. In history, an ancient Roman held up a scroll that suddenly looked like a bottle of ketchup. In art, the crimson oil paint reminded him of tomato soup.

Phil knew Keely was really excited about visiting Ketchup World. She was bound to be disappointed if he begged off with the "allergy" excuse. But he couldn't think of a solution to his problem. So, when the last bell rang, Phil went straight home to talk to his parents.

"You really want to go to this Pickford

Ranch?" Mr. Diffy asked. He was sitting on the family room couch, looking over the permission form Phil had handed him.

"Yeah, I do," replied Phil, pacing back and forth. "You know, every time I start to feel like a normal kid from a normal family, *something* gets in the way. Like this—"

Phil plopped down on the couch. He yanked off his sneaker, pulled off his sock, and banged his bare foot down on the coffee table.

"Sweetie," said Mrs. Diffy from her easy chair, "if you're concerned that your feet smell, just do what your dad does."

Mr. Diffy nodded. "Half hour in a vinegar soak, then dust them with cornmeal!"

Phil rolled his eyes. "It's not the *smell*, Mom. I'm talking about how people in this century have *five* toes. Not four."

Mr. and Mrs. Diffy exchanged a silent look, then burst out in peals of laughter.

"Oh!" cried Mr. Diffy, doubling over.

"That's right!" shrieked Mrs. Diffy, chuckling

like crazy. "They won't lose their pinkie toe for seventy-five years!"

Mr. Diffy shook his head. "How do they walk with all those things?"

Mrs. Diffy picked up a cheese puff from a snack bowl. She held it next to the fourth toe on her bare foot. "*Hello.* I am a useless pinkie toe," she said in a French accent while making the little orange puff dance. "Some day you will be born without me. Ha, ha, ha."

Phil sighed. "Guys, I'm *serious.*" But clearly his parents weren't. In fact, they might have kept laughing all evening if Pim hadn't interrupted them.

"Okay, family, I don't have much time for chitchat," she announced, marching into the family room. "I need donations. Watches, necklaces, belt buckles, gold fillings. Don't be stingy. It's for a good cause."

Pim walked around the room, holding out a tall cardboard box. A sign on it read SAVE MR. HACKETT. Mr. Diffy dropped a wad of cash into the box. Phil tossed in his wristwatch. And Mrs. Diffy contributed her ring and bracelet.

When her collecting was finished, Pim stared at her family. "Thank you," she said in a monotone. "Your donations are appreciated. I'm touched, et cetera, et cetera."

As far as Pim was concerned, doing charity work was one thing. Being all cheerful and chipper about it was another. Pim did not—repeat, *did not*—do chipper and cheerful. With a roll of her eyes, she marched off to her bedroom to calculate the take.

After Pim had gone, Mr. Diffy turned to Phil. "Son, if you really want to go on this field trip, I'm going to find a way to get you there."

Phil brightened. "Really?" He didn't think his parents were going to understand how completely *major* this problem was.

His mother still didn't quite get it. Chuckling, she turned to her husband. "What are you going to do? Build him falsies?"

"Yes," said Mr. Diffy with a frown. Just

because I can't fix our time-travel machine, he thought, doesn't mean I can't build my son a couple of phony body parts!

Mrs. Diffy stopped chuckling.

For the rest of the afternoon, Phil's father turned his backyard into a toe-making shop. In 2121, Mr. Diffy liked to sculpt with Pliable Polymers. But they hadn't been invented yet. So he was stuck with early twenty-first-century technology. Luckily for him, the Hobby Time Channel had just done an entire series called *Plaster Is Your Friend*.

First, Phil's father created a cast of two fake little toes—one for the right foot and one for the left. After they set, he unmolded them. Then he painted the toes a flesh color and applied fake toenails. Finally, he gave them piggy-toe manicures . . . and *voilà*! Phil's fake fifth toes were ready to go!

"Phil!" Mr. Diffy called excitedly through the back door. "It's toe time!"

CHAPTER THREE

In her own mind, Pim was a goddess and a genius. She figured it was only a matter of time before some civilization put her on a throne. Until then, she vowed to make the best use of her talents—wherever and *whenever* she happened to be.

At the moment, she was standing in a crowded H.G. Wells hallway, trying to make a fund-raising sale before the late-bell rang. It shouldn't be that hard, she told herself. What was that old twenty-first-century saying? *There's a sucker born every minute.*

Pim wholeheartedly agreed. She also agreed with that saying from her own time: "Profits are spelled s-u-c-k-e-r-s in my business!" Okay, so the guy who said it was the inventor of the Eternal Lollipop. But what the heck, thought Pim, it seems appropriate enough for *my* work today.

"Pssst," she whispered to a short boy in a Hawaiian shirt. "Yeah, you," she confirmed when he glanced up at her with wide, innocent, *gullible* eyes.

Excellent, she thought, I've used my superior abilities to choose the perfect dupe. Now all I have to do is reel him in.

Pim smiled as her sucker walked over. "What's your name?" she asked.

"Jorge," he replied.

"Jorge, what would you say if I could put you in a big, fancy belt buckle?" she asked, then quickly added, "Don't answer. Just step into my *jacket*."

Pim opened up her long, black leather jacket.

Inside, clipped to the lining, she'd hung watches, rings, belt buckles, calculators, cell phones, and a variety of other items.

Jorge gawked at Pim's walking mini-mall.

"Or would you like a gold locket?" she offered.

Jorge shook his head. "No, thanks."

The boy was about to leave, but Pim blocked his exit. "Jorge, did I mention it's for a teacher getting a nasty operation? None of the money goes to me."

Pim was pleased to see Jorge's eyes widening with interest. "Really?" he asked.

"Well, I did buy myself a prime rib sandwich at lunch," she confessed. The way Pim saw it, the Hackett fund *owed* her a delicious meal after all her hard work. "But that's on the down low," she told Jorge. "You know what I'm saying? Huh?" She laughed and poked his shoulder.

Jorge frowned. He thought Pim was cute but she was just *too* weird. "I have to be somewhere else now," he said quickly, then bolted down the hall.

"Yeah, right," said Pim bitterly. Another sucker lost, she thought.

But Pim wasn't about to give up. Not with Debbie Berwick trying to prove that she, Sally Sunshine, was the better fund-raiser.

"Hey, you with the face," called Pim, spotting a brand-new sucker, "come here!"

While Pim continued to flash her wearable mini-mall to kids on the second floor of the school, Debbie peddled goody baskets on the first floor.

"Fun Baskets, five dollars! Get your Fun Baskets, five dollars!" she cried with bouncy enthusiasm. "It's for a really good cause!"

A table filled with wicker baskets stood in the middle of the busy hallway. Debbie had filled each one with candies and goodies—all donated by grocery-store managers she'd visited the day before. Then she'd wrapped each basket in colorful cellophane and tied it with a ribbon.

"Oh! Hi, Morton," Debbie called to a popular upperclassman. "Let me tell you a little bit about today's fund-raiser. I'm raising money for a teacher who's very, very sick." She made a big show of frowning and shook her head with grave sadness. "It doesn't look good."

Morton sighed guiltily. "All right," he said and handed her a five-dollar bill.

"Thank you, Morton!" Debbie exclaimed, passing him a yellow basket. "You're good people."

Morton smiled. "Thanks, Debbie."

"Fun Baskets!" Debbie continued to call. She noticed her sister-in-fund-raising walking by. "Hi, Pim!"

Pim glanced at Debbie's elaborate display of colorfully wrapped baskets. *Yikes*, she thought, what did Sally Sunshine do—make an off-season deal with the Easter bunny?

"My baskets are really moving," Debbie chirped. "How much have *you* raised?"

Pim's eyes narrowed. "Squat," she snapped. "Leave me alone." Then she turned on her heel to find a brand-new sucker-detecting spot.

To Phil Diffy, twenty-first-century yellow school buses were totally *archaic*—clunky, loud, and drafty. But they were also very cool, like rolling museums. On any other day, Phil would have enjoyed the bus ride out to Pickford Ranch. Today, however, he was too worried to enjoy anything.

After leaving the suburbs, the bus had turned onto a lonely country road. Farmland stretched for miles. The kids around him were all having a great time. Dressed casually in T-shirts and shorts, they laughed and talked.

But not Phil. The whole way, he just stared out the window and kept wiping nervous sweat off his palms. Whoa, he thought, this fake pinkie toe thing is totally wrecking me.

Earlier that morning, he'd attached his new fake toes to his feet. Then he'd tested them out by pacing back and forth on his bedroom carpet. At first, he thought everything was going to work out fine.

My feet actually look like they have *five* toes, he told himself. Now I'll look like all the other humans from this time period.

But then he put on his socks and shoes. Inside the tight confines of his sneakers, the fifth toes felt funny—like giant rocks in his shoes. He kept losing his balance and tripping. So he pulled off the toes and tucked them safely into the pocket of his shorts.

I'll just wait until I get to the tomato ranch, he told himself. When the time is right, I'll glue on the toes again. But what if I don't get the chance?

"We're almost there!" Keely exclaimed from the seat next to him. She pointed out the school bus window. On a green rolling hill, a huge billboard read:

Pickford Ranch
Join our Ketchup Days celebration!
Historical re-creation of the early years
of Pickford. Just five miles away.
Come stomp with us!

Keely grinned and pointed to her feet. Phil wiped beads of sweat off his forehead and forced himself to return her smile.

A few minutes later, the bus pulled into the Pickford Ranch parking lot. On one side of the lot there was a modern factory. On the other side was a quaint, small town. The little village looked the same as it had in the nineteenth century.

Phil followed his classmates off the bus and into the "historic" area. Banjo music played over loudspeakers as a tour guide showed them around "Old Pickford." There were rustic wooden buildings, horse-drawn carts, and people dressed in Old West costumes. Balloons and colorful KETCHUP DAYS banners were everywhere.

Finally, the students were led to a huge wooden cask.

Wow, thought Phil, that's either the tomato-stomping vat or the largest hot tub I've *ever* seen.

Just then, a tall, skinny man stepped onto a

low stage next to a weathered barn. The man wore a coonskin cap, garters on the arms of his pin-striped shirt, and a red ribbon tie. A gold watch chain hung from the pocket of his old-fashioned vest.

He adjusted his round, wire-rimmed glasses and tapped on a microphone. When the kids looked up, he waved them over. The man introduced himself as Mr. Fleet and welcomed them to Pickford Ranch. Then he launched into the same spiel he gave to all the visiting tourists.

"Tomato pioneer Ira Pickford never did find the gold he was looking for. But he did find another treasure. Red gold. The pride of Pickford." Mr. Fleet reached down and picked up his favorite prop—a tomato. "From this humble fruit flows the most noble of meat sauces . . . ketchup!"

With an excited nod, Keely turned to Phil and poked his arm. He forced a smile as he put a hand in his pocket. *Phew*, he thought. His two fake little toes were still there. Any moment now, he'd go somewhere and glue them on.

Mr. Fleet held the tomato up for all to see. He continued his speech, his voice quivering with emotion. "This town was built on the hard work and sweaty back of a man . . . with a *dream*."

Misty-eyed, Mr. Fleet looked off into the distance. The kids impatiently glanced at each other, waiting for the man to get on with it.

Phil pumped his fist in the air. "So, let's get to stompin', huh!" he declared.

Keely turned to him. "I thought you were allergic to tomatoes."

Phil's eyes darted back and forth nervously. "Yeah, I got my allergy shot last night," he said, trying to sound convincing.

"Right," said Keely, scratching her head. She didn't know what Phil's problem was—but she suspected he definitely had one. And it wasn't allergies. He'd hardly said two words to her on the long bus ride. Now, suddenly, he was acting very enthusiastic.

"All right!" Mr. Fleet finally announced. "Everyone please remove your shoes and socks!"

All the kids hit the ground and stripped down to their bare feet. Phil stood like a statue in the center of the frenzied activity, stunned.

Everyone's changing right out in the *open*, he realized in panic.

"Excuse me," he called to Mr. Fleet, "is there a place I can change?"

"Change?" Keely cried from the ground. "We're just taking off our shoes and socks."

Mr. Fleet gave Phil a kind smile. "Oddly enough, for some of our shier visitors, we *do* have changing facilities." He pointed to a wooden screen a few yards away.

Phil darted behind it. Close one, he thought, as he pulled the fake little toes out of his pocket. Using the special biochemical glue his father had invented, he attached the toes to his bare feet.

Lookin' *good*, he thought, checking out his

new five-toed feet. When he was fairly sure the glue had dried, he peeked out from behind the screen. All of his classmates were now stomping around in the giant tomato vat.

Okay, he thought, guess it's time to make my *toe*-mato debut!

With confidence, Phil strode over to the big wooden tub. He'd worn shorts, like most of the kids, so he didn't have to roll up his pant legs. He just climbed up the ladder and stepped right into the shallow pool of thick, red goop.

All the kids were laughing as they stomped around the vat. The only person who didn't look very happy was Keely.

"Hey," she said. The bounce was gone from her voice. And she seemed kind of annoyed with him.

"Hey, there," Phil replied. She turned to stomp away, but he quickly caught up to her. "So, uh, you may have noticed I've been acting a little weird lately."

"Now that you mention it," she said. "A little."

"Yeah." Phil cleared his throat. He hadn't meant to spoil the field trip for her. "I'm sorry about that."

"It's okay," said Keely. "So, are you back to being *normal Phil* again?"

Phil nodded enthusiastically. "So normal it hurts."

Keely smiled. Phil smiled back. They happily stomped in place.

"Phil, you want to go to the deep end?" Keely asked after a minute.

"No," Phil snapped, suddenly tense. "I *don't* want to go to the deep end. I'm fine right *here*. Thanks. Can you just leave me alone for a minute?"

Keely glared at her friend, totally stung. She couldn't *believe* he was being so rude—and after he'd promised to act normal again! "*Whatever*, Phil," she told him, then stomped away.

Phil knew he'd just hurt Keely's feelings. But, at the moment, he couldn't do anything about it. He was *frantic*. Somewhere in all the thick, red tomato goop, one of his fake little toes had fallen off!

"Where's my toe?" he moaned.

CHAPTER FOUR

This can't be happening, Phil said to himself. He bent over and started swishing his hands through the tomato soup. But his fake toe had completely disappeared.

I must not have waited long enough for the glue to dry! he realized.

He searched behind him, in front of him, and then to the side. "Excuse me," he said after bumping into a kid. "I lost my wallet."

At the other end of the large tub, Keely was still steaming. "I swear Phil Diffy has more mood swings than my mother," she growled to a blond boy from her band class. "I mean, have you noticed that? He's up, he's down. If you want to be his friend, I'm telling ya, *strap in*."

The blond boy obviously didn't want to get involved. He gave Keely a shrug that said, "Hey, not my business," and hurriedly moved away from her.

Meanwhile, back in the shallow end, Phil was still fishing for his lost appendage. His hand brushed against something. "Ewww," he murmured with a shudder. He hadn't found his toe. He'd found something even more disturbing—a used Band-Aid. He tossed the disgusting thing out of the vat and went back to raking his fingers through the muck. "Where's my toe?" he mumbled.

Just then, Mr. Fleet shouted at the top of his lungs, "Your attention, please! Nobody move! We've detected a foreign article in the slurry."

Phil froze. *Uh-oh*, he thought. At the other end of the vat, it seemed that Mr. Fleet had spotted Phil's wayward toe. The Pickford tour guide climbed into the tub of tomatoes with a pair of silver tongs.

He's about to grab it! Phil realized with horror. He pictured his principal making the entire class stand side by side in a barefoot lineup. Everyone would finally see that Phil was a four-toed freak from the twenty-second century!

Phil knew he had to do something, but what? *Distraction*, he decided. Reaching down, his fingers closed around one of the whole tomatoes still floating in the goop. Holding it like a squishy red baseball, he hurled it across the tub at Mr. Fleet. But just as the tomato was about to hit him, the man bent down. The red fruit flew past the tour guide, heading right for the face of the girl standing behind him—Keely!

Whap!

For a second, Keely just stood there, stunned, her mouth hanging open. Phil Diffy, she thought, over the past few days you have been weird, moody, and just plain rude. But this is the *last* straw. Narrowing her eyes, she reached down and grabbed another whole tomato. *Take that!* she thought as she threw it right at him.

Phil ducked, and the tomato hit the blond kid from Keely's band class square in the chest. *Squish!*

The blond kid laughed and threw a tomato back at Keely. Instead, it hit Mr. Fleet right in his arm. *Bam!*

The next thing Phil knew, a tomato fight had broken out. The "Pride of Pickford" was flying all over the place. *Squish! Squash! Splat!* Mr. Fleet was caught in the middle—and he was *not* very happy about it.

After a few minutes of chaos, Phil grabbed a big, ripe tomato. He raised his arm high for the windup—and felt steely fingers close around his wrist. When he turned to look, he found the school principal holding his arm tight.

Uh-oh, thought Phil.

The man's face was red, but not from getting hit with tomatoes. The principal was furious.

Seeing him, the other kids stopped throwing tomatoes, and Mr. Fleet cried, "All right! Everybody out of the tub!"

The principal himself escorted Phil across the lawn and toward the school bus. Mr. Fleet saw them and marched over.

"There's always one bad tomato in every vat!" Mr. Fleet cried. He took off his tomato-stained coonskin cap and shook its ratty tail right under Phil's nose. "You can explain it to your principal!"

"Fun Baskets, five dollars! Get your Fun Baskets!" Back at school, Debbie Berwick was still at it. "They're for a good cause! Fun Baskets! Get your Fun Baskets!"

Pim was sick of hearing Debbie peddling her fund-raiser baskets between classes. Okay, she told herself, no more playing. It's time for some *serious* fund-raising!

For the rest of the afternoon, Pim went after her targets with total ruthlessness. There was a boy in her math class who was so tense that he broke his pencil in two. While the teacher wasn't looking, she raced over to his desk.

"*Oh*, and right during the biggest test of the semester," she whispered. "Luckily, I have a sweet number two for sale. Let's call it six bucks even."

The boy sighed as he dug into his pants pocket. Pim's asking price for a new pencil would empty his wallet, but he needed it. So he handed over the cash.

A little later, Pim went to the gym to look for more victims. She found her first one on the wrestling mat—underneath an opponent.

"Hi," she told him brightly, kneeling down on the mat next to him, "I couldn't help but notice you're getting *smoked*. How about a nice scented candle to lift your spirits?"

The wrestler moaned as the referee ended the match. The boy stared at Pim. For some reason, the ridiculous candle actually did lift his spirits. He reached out for it.

"That'll be three-fifty," Pim informed him.

Her next fund-raising location was the biggest success of all—the girls' lavatory. Pim wasn't surprised. After all, she thought, once you've locked yourself in a stall, you aren't exactly in a position to walk away from a sales pitch.

"Cheryl, I know you're a little *occupado* right now," Pim called into one of the closed stalls, "but these never need winding." She slid a tray of watches underneath the locked door. "Don't rush!"

At the end of the school day, Pim and Debbie met in an empty classroom. They counted up their earnings, then went looking for Mr. Hackett. They found him sitting behind the big desk in his office.

Debbie started off the presentation. Approaching her teacher's desk, she announced, "I'm going to say this quickly, otherwise I'm going to start crying."

"Here we go with the tears," muttered Pim. She handed Debbie a tissue. Okay, Pim admitted to herself, so the tissue's a little used. But it's the thought that counts.

"We want you to have this money," Debbie finally told Mr. Hackett, dabbing tears from her eyes. She held her fund-raising jar out to him. "It's one hundred and ten dollars."

"*My* jar is one hundred and *fifteen* dollars," noted Pim, holding out her own jar. Oh, yes, she thought. I *am* the superior fund-raiser. *Go, Pimmy! Go, Pimmy! Go!*

Mr. Hackett politely took the girls' jars. "So, this is wonderful. Thank you," he told them sincerely. Then he stared at the jars in complete confusion. "Why on Earth would you be doing this?"

"Cut the hero act," said Pim. "We know about the operation."

Mr. Hackett's eyes widened in surprise. "You do?"

"Yes," said Debbie, ringing her hands, "and

we want you to be brave and know that we support you."

"I can see that," said the teacher.

Debbie bit her lower lip. "Are you scared?"

"A little. Thank you," said Mr. Hackett. After all, he thought, I don't know what my new hair will actually *look* like.

Pim and Debbie gave their teacher one last encouraging smile, then they turned and left. Mr. Hackett shook the jars of loot.

Ka-ching, ka-ching!

"I love public service!" he declared with delight.

The Pickford Ranch field trip was officially over. But before the kids returned to school, the principal had called out a dozen names. He was going to give detention to every student he'd seen throwing tomatoes in the stomping tub.

By now, a long line of guilty tomato throwers had already been to the principal's office. Phil sat on a bench outside, awaiting his turn. He flipped through one magazine, then another. After an hour, Phil and the blond kid from Keely's band class were the only ones left to go.

"All right, Johnson!" the principal bellowed from inside his office. "You're next! Get in here!"

Phil sighed as he watched the blond kid disappear behind the office door. He picked up yet another magazine. When he saw an advertisement for Pickford Ranch ketchup, he shuddered and tossed it aside.

Just then, a familiar voice announced: "Sometimes, I dream I'm married to Mr. Potato Head."

Excuse me? Phil thought. He looked up to find Keely standing there. She was still wearing her field trip clothes. Tomato stains covered her from head to foot.

". . . and we live in a two-bedroom condo in Boca Raton, Florida," she continued.

Phil blinked. "What?"

"And I want to be a doctor," she added, "but

he wants me to stay home and take care of our five spuds."

Phil shook his head in confusion. "So, why are you telling me this?"

"Because it's my deepest, darkest secret. And because I know what's going on." She sat down next to him on the bench and pulled something out of her pocket. "I found this in the goop."

Phil's eyes widened at the sight of his lost little toe. "What? That's not mine," he said quickly.

Keely squinted at the teeny, tiny writing on the bottom. "'Property of P. Diffy,'" she read.

Phil gulped.

"You have four toes," Keely guessed. "So what. You don't have to hide things from me."

"Really?" he asked.

"Yeah," she said. "You've spent the last three days lying and acting all weird, and throwing tomatoes at me, just because of a *pinkie toe*?"

"It does feel kind of good to get my toe off my chest," he admitted.

Keely sighed with relief. "Phil, you're my *best* friend. Just promise me no more secrets. You and I are on a one-hundred-percent honesty pact. Deal?"

"Deal," Phil promised.

Keely rose to leave, and Phil suddenly felt guilty. He had just promised his best friend that he wouldn't keep any more secrets from her. Yet he was still keeping the biggest secret of his life.

"Wait," he called as she walked away. He stood up. "There's one more thing."

Keely turned and walked back. "What is it?" she asked. With a reassuring smile, she added, "Don't worry."

Phil cleared his throat. What he was about to do was extremely risky. Even dangerous. If Keely freaked, there was no telling what might happen to him and his family.

But I trust her, Phil thought. I care about our friendship. And how can our friendship survive if I keep trying to hide things from her?

"The reason why I have four toes," he

confessed, "is because . . . where I'm from, *everyone* does."

Keely's brow furrowed in confusion. She obviously didn't understand what he was trying to say.

"I grew up over a hundred years from now," Phil finally admitted. "I'm from the future."

CHAPTER FIVE

"I'm telling you, Maurice, I am *loved* here!" Mr. Hackett exclaimed. The teacher sat in his office chair with a big, plastic barber's apron draped around him—and a huge smile splitting his face.

Behind him, the hairdresser Maurice stood working on Hackett's bald head. He was halfway through attaching an elaborate toupee.

"Students are standing in line to hand me jars of money," the teacher continued to boast, "which is, of course, what allowed me to upgrade to the two-eleven."

Just then, Debbie and Pim walked back into the office. "Excuse us, Mr. Hackett," Debbie began, "but we wanted to wish you good luck on—" She broke off suddenly. "*What* is growing out of your head?"

Pim took in the hairdresser, plastic apron, and salon equipment. She added up the evidence in a heartbeat. "Wait a minute," she snapped. "*That's* your operation? I busted my hump so you could get a *wig*."

"It's not a wig," corrected Mr. Hackett. "It's the Lorenzo Lamas."

The teacher picked up a big hand mirror. He held it up to admire the bushy head of brown hair now crowning his forehead. *Sweet*, he thought, I am so . . . hairy!

Debbie frowned. "No disrespect, Mr. Hackett," she said, "but I'm going to have to give my money to a needier charity."

"Yeah, ditto," said Pim. "I'm giving mine

to the 'Pim-Diffy-Needs-a-High-Definition-TV Foundation.'" Both girls grabbed their money jars, turned on their heels, and walked out of the office.

Pim couldn't believe the teacher had taken their money in the first place. "You disgust me," she muttered on her way out.

"Wait a minute!" Mr. Hackett called after them. "How am I supposed to pay for this?"

Uh-oh, he thought, as Maurice's hands suddenly pulled away from his head.

"I mean, Maurice, I can pay for this," Mr. Hackett quickly promised. "Just, you know, maybe not all at once. What are you doing? Don't get quiet on me, Maurice. Don't leave! Maurice!"

But it was too late. The hairdresser had packed up all of his materials and marched out the door. With a sigh, Mr. Hackett held up the hand mirror and examined his head. Maurice had only finished half of the toupee.

Goodness, Mr. Hackett thought, the front of

my head looks better than any of the "after" pictures in those hair-replacement ads. But the back looks worse than before!

"I'm only half a Lamas," he said with a groan.

Meanwhile, in another part of the school, Phil was still trying to explain to Keely.

". . . So we were taking our vacation visiting the prehistoric era," he explained, pacing back and forth in front of her. "There were cavemen and dinosaurs, but—*whatever!*—my dad had to go back to work. So we swung by the French Revolution and headed for home. Then our time machine broke down. So now we're stuck here in your time."

By now, Keely had dropped back down onto the bench. She stared at Phil in shock as he continued his story. "According to my dad, if the government found out, we'd be captured, or worse."

Phil waited for Keely to say something. To

ask a question, maybe. To make a joke. But she said nothing. She just continued to stare at him, her jaw slack.

"Uh. If you can hear me, can you nod or something?" asked Phil.

"Diffy!" yelled the principal from inside his office. "Get in here! Your turn!"

Phil sighed as he approached the man's door. He looked back at Keely. She rose from her seat and began to back away from him. She *still* hadn't said a word.

One more time, Phil tried to get through. "I just wanted my best friend to know the truth about me."

But Keely just kept backing away. And before Phil had even set foot inside the principal's office, she was gone.

"You told her *what?*" Mr. Diffy roared after dinner that evening. "Why?"

Phil faced his father on the back porch. He'd just confessed what he'd told Keely. "I had to," he said. "She told me she has dreams about being married to Mr. Potato Head."

"What?" Mr. Diffy put a hand to his forehead. He suddenly looked like he was going to be ill.

"It's Keely's innermost secret," Phil explained. "And when she told me, I realized that it doesn't matter what century you're from. Real friends are truthful with each other. And I need a friend. A *real* friend."

Mr. Diffy didn't see it that way. He held his head and paced around the porch in a frantic circle. "Phil, Phil, Phil, Phil, Phil! When this leaks out, there are going to be news reports and a manhunt! Before you know it, they're going to be busting down our door."

Just then, the gate of their backyard fence began to violently rattle. It sounded as if someone was trying to break into their property!

"Mama Lukes!" cried Mr. Diffy. "Did you hear that? They're here!"

But when the gate opened, a pretty, blond,

teenage girl walked through. "Hey," Keely called, waving to Phil and his father. She walked up to the back porch. "Sorry about the racket. Your gate sticks a bit."

Just then, Mrs. Diffy walked outside. "Hey," she called to her husband and son. "I thought I heard someone at the gate."

"Oh, it's just me, Mrs. Diffy." Keely smiled and held up a plate of homemade brownies. "I never officially welcomed you to the neighborhood."

"Aw, thank you, Keely," said Mrs. Diffy, accepting the gift. "Although we do miss Lawrence, Kansas," she recited in a practiced voice, "geographical center of the nation!"

"Save it," grumbled Mr. Diffy. "Our son spilled the beans."

Mrs. Diffy's happy face dropped. "I'll go pack," she told him and headed for the back door.

That's when Keely spoke up. "Phil, I don't care if you're from the future—"

Mrs. Diffy stopped and turned to listen.

"Or from Kansas, or some nut job from . . . Nutsville," Keely continued. "It doesn't matter to me. Whatever secrets you have, they're safe with me."

"Thank you. That really means a lot to me," Phil said softly. He exchanged a look with his mom and dad. "It means a lot to *us*."

Mr. Diffy suddenly felt sorry he'd doubted his son's decision to trust his best friend. But he knew a way to make it up to him. "Phil, it looks like your new friend might want a ride home." With a smile, Mr. Diffy pulled a Skyak orb out of his pants pocket.

Phil's face brightened at the sight of the glowing sphere. "Really?" he asked.

Mr. Diffy nodded and tossed the orb into the air. Phil caught it with one hand. He smiled at Keely, then rolled it out onto the backyard lawn.

On the grass, the glowing orb began to blink. With a brilliant flash of light, it expanded and shaped itself into something that looked like a squat, purple snowmobile. Phil climbed onto the vehicle's seat and pulled on his helmet.

"Ohmigosh, Phil!" Keely whispered in awe. "You really are from the future."

Phil held out a helmet. "It's a Skyak. Hop on."

Keely climbed onto the seat behind Phil and strapped on her helmet.

"Be careful," called Mrs. Diffy.

Phil waved to his parents. Then he revved the Skyak's motor and lifted off.

Mr. Diffy put an arm around his wife's shoulders as they watched Phil and Keely zoom away.

"Aw, honey," Mrs. Diffy said with a wistful sigh, "remember our first Skyak ride?"

Mr. Diffy blinked in confusion. "I never had a Skyak."

Oops, thought Mrs. Diffy.

High above them, Phil had never been happier. Racing through the starry night on a Skyak had always rocked. But having Keely with him made it a thousand times better.

"Phil," whispered Keely, "this is a little scary."

Welcome to *my* world, thought Phil.

Fitting into the twenty-first century wasn't easy. And sometimes it was a little frightening. But one thing definitely made it *less* of a horror show—having a friend like Keely watching your back.

Turning in his seat, Phil gave his best friend a reassuring smile. "Hold on," he said. "Everything will be just fine."

The next day, Pim was sitting in Mr. Hackett's class, trying to pay attention. It wasn't easy. His new wig was really distracting. It looked like a small forest animal had decided to take a nap on his head.

"That's right, Debbie," the teacher was saying, "the Dust Bowl ripped through the state of Oklahoma. Once a fertile land, which was covered in lush crops and fields, the Dust Bowl left behind a dry, barren wasteland, where nothing would grow."

Mr. Hackett turned around to write something on the chalkboard, and the entire class screamed with laughter. Hackett's new hair only covered the *front* half of his head. The back was as bald as ever.

Yikes, thought Pim, staring. Did he just say something about a barren wasteland where nothing would grow?

The teacher spun around to face the class. The kids instantly shut up. Once more, he turned toward the chalkboard. And again the kids laughed like crazy.

With a sigh, Mr. Hackett gave up. Until he could afford to pay Maurice for the rest of the hair transplant, there was really nothing he could do. "Okay," he told the hysterical class. "Enjoy."

Pim exchanged a smile with Debbie—and then a high five. In the end, Pim figured that collecting donations for a charity really wasn't so hard. In fact, it was kind of fun. If only Mr. Hackett had been honest and given back the money.

Oh, well, thought Pim, I guess that's what happens when you turn a fund-raising drive into a *hair-raising* experience.

PART TWO

CHAPTER ONE

"**N**ext up, Keely Teslow!" called a bouncy voice from inside the H.G. Wells gymnasium.

Cheerleading tryouts were closed to spectators. But Phil Diffy didn't care. When he heard Keely's name called, he cracked open the gym's heavy door and peeked through.

Keely looked totally psyched as she bounded down the bleachers. She flashed the judges a wide grin, then took her place in the middle of the polished wood floor.

"All right, Keely, show us what you got," said the squad's captain.

From the crack in the door, Phil watched Keely nod and count off, "Five, six, seven, eight . . ."

"Come on, Keely, you can do it," he whispered.

She started with a few dance steps. Then she jumped high, did a split leap, and went into her tumbling.

"Ooh, nice cartwheel," whispered Phil. "And another . . . and another . . ." *Whoa,* he thought, as she reached the end of the gym's main floor. "That's plenty, Keely . . . watch out for the—"

Crash!

"Sorry," Keely called to the judges.

Phil shuddered, backed away, and let the door close again. Some things were just too painful to watch.

Twenty minutes later, the tryouts were over. Two girls ran out of the gym holding pom-poms. When they reached the hall, they stopped, squealed, and hugged each other. More girls came out. Some looked deliriously happy, others looked utterly dejected. Finally, Phil saw

Keely. Her shoulders were slumped, her eyes downcast.

"So, how'd it go?" he asked, even though he already knew.

Keely shrugged. "I was doing great. Unfortunately, a vending machine got in my way." She held out a candy bar for him. It was one of the dozens that had come tumbling out of the machine after she'd crashed into it. "I don't even think a Señor Nougat will cheer me up."

Phil took the candy. Señor Nougat was one of his favorites—*almost* as good as the twenty-second-century candy called Mockberry Chew. "I'm sorry you didn't make the squad, Keel."

"Thanks," she said with a sigh. "I guess I'll get over it . . . but I'm not sure *someone else* I know will."

"Oh, yeah. Who's that?" Phil asked.

Before Keely could answer, a short, blond woman in a red business suit came rushing up to them. She had a huge grin on her face and an enormous flower wreath in her hands. A silk ribbon draped across the wreath read "Congrat-ulations!"

"Oh, my sweet, luscious love muffin!" cried Keely's mother as she hung the wreath around her daughter's neck. "So, what's the good news?"

Keely's eyes widened in panic. "I . . ." she began, but her voice suddenly died off. She glanced at Phil for moral support. He gave her an encouraging nod. Then she looked wor-riedly back at her mother. Mrs. Teslow's face suddenly tensed, as if the world was about to end.

"I . . . *made* it," Keely said. "Yeah, I'm a cheerleader."

"Oh! I knew it!" Mrs. Teslow exclaimed. She pulled her daughter into a choking bear hug. "Oh, darling, I'm so proud of you!"

Phil blinked. He stood frozen for a second, wondering why on Earth Keely had just lied to her mother.

"Phil, you little pumpkin-head, get in this

hug," said Mrs. Teslow, pulling him into the clench. "Oh! This is the happiest day of my life. Oh, it is!"

Phil glanced at Keely, but she quickly shook her head. "Don't say anything," she mouthed silently as her mother continued exclaiming, "Ooooooh!"

Later that day, the results of the cheerleading tryouts were broadcast during the school's televised announcements. Phil's sister Pim watched on a closed-circuit TV in Mr. Hackett's classroom as Seth Wosmer, that day's anchor, wrapped up his broadcast. "So, at the assembly, the principal will give an important peach—" Seth paused and blinked. "I meant, *speech*. Speech!"

Pim rolled her eyes. What a loser, she thought. "Now would be a great time for a fire drill," she whispered to Debbie Berwick in the next row.

Debbie ignored Pim's crack. "I just *love*

watching the news!" she gushed. "One day, I hope to be an Action News anchor."

"You've got the mouth for it," Pim muttered.

"And that wraps it up. I'm Seth Wosmer." Forcing a lopsided grin, Seth flung up his arm to wave good-bye and knocked over the water glass sitting in front of him. *Wham!* "Aw, chunks!" he exclaimed. Then he tried to wipe up the spill with his Action News script.

At the front of the classroom, Mr. Hackett shook his head. "I knew he was going to choke big-time," he murmured, then clicked off the TV. With a sigh, the teacher rose from his chair. "Okay, people, before we get to our lesson, I have some work sheets to hand out. So I will need a volun—" Mr. Hackett jumped in surprise. Debbie Berwick had suddenly appeared right next to him. "—teer." He hadn't even seen the girl cross the room! "I don't know how you do that, Debbie," said Mr. Hackett, "but it's mildly creepy."

Pim instantly appeared at the teacher's other

side. "Aaah!" he cried, jumping again. What is this? he thought. Revenge of the teacher's pets? Are they *trying* to give me a heart attack?

"I'll pass out those work sheets," Pim announced. She pulled the stack of papers from his hands. "I think we all agree it's time Debbie Berwick sat one out."

"Oh, no!" cried Debbie. She lunged to pull the work sheets back. "That's okay. I love to volunteer. Really. It makes my heart glow!"

"'*I love to volunteer. It makes my heart glow,*'" Pim repeated, struggling to keep her grip on the stack of papers. *Arrrgh!* she thought. The glare from Debbie's sunny attitude is giving me a blinding headache! "Berwick, you keep pushing my buttons!"

"Look, I'm the teacher. I'm the one with the buttons." Mr. Hackett yanked the work sheets away from the grappling girls and split the pile in two. "You can *both* hand out the work sheets."

Pim grabbed her half and went toe-to-toe

with Debbie. "You can't win, Berwick. You know that."

But Debbie held tightly to her own half and just kept smiling.

"Okay, you two, it's not a competition," the teacher warned. "Go."

Like racehorses out of the gate, the two girls took off. Pim rushed toward the left side of the room, Debbie the right.

"Careful," warned Mr. Hackett. "Slow down. . . ."

But the girls only sped up. They galloped down one aisle and up another, slapping down work sheet after work sheet. *Wham! Bam! Slam!*

"Hey!" Mr. Hackett called to them. "No running in the classroom!"

But Pim and Debbie were on a mission. Each wanted to finish passing out her sheets *first*. Students reared back in fear as the girls slapped papers onto their desks.

"Slow down!" cried Mr. Hackett. "Hey!"

Too late. Pim and Debbie were so crazed, they didn't notice that their paths were about to converge. . . .

"Whoa, whoa, whoa . . . aaah!" the teacher exclaimed as Pim and Debbie slammed into each other.

Both girls ended up on the floor. Papers fluttered down on them like confetti. Mr. Hackett leaned over the girls. "Okay!" he cried, forming a time-out T with his hands. "Issue resolution. Counselor's office. Right now."

Neither Pim nor Debbie had ever seen the school counselor. The two unhappily trudged down the hall to his office and picked up an appointment slip from his secretary.

An hour later, they walked through the counselor's door and approached his desk. The man in the desk chair had his back to them. As they drew closer, he spun around to face them.

"Mr. Hackett?" Debbie asked in surprise.

The balding teacher gave the girls a laid-back smile. "Oh, don't think of me as Mr. Hackett, uptight schoolteacher," he told them. "No. In here, I'm Neal Hackett, easygoing counselor." He pointed to his clothes. His brown corduroy suit jacket was gone. In its place was a forest green cardigan. "See? Warm, fuzzy sweater." He smiled again. "So. What's the *problemo*?"

"Um. First of all," Debbie began, "I would like to say that since I *love* you as a teacher, I know I'm going to *love* you as a counselor!"

As Debbie excitedly clapped her hands together, Pim blew her stack. "That's the *problemo*!" she yelled. "She loves everything. She loves homework! She loves earwax! She loves—"

Mr. Hackett held up his hand. "Pim, I hear where you're coming from, and I can totally roll with that. But what do you say we dial it down a notch, hey? *Grazie*."

Pim sighed. "Mr. Hackett, all I'm saying is, it's not natural to *love* everything."

"Pim, I disagree," Debbie said calmly. "But I *love* that you voice your opinion."

Pim's fists clenched in fury.

"Okay," Mr. Hackett said, throwing up his hands. "Well, we can go round and round on this one, but what's the point in that, hmm? So, why don't you two just go on back to class because Neal here's got some *school business* to attend to."

From under his desk, the man pulled out a bright blue Boogie board. He didn't want to be late for his weekly meeting with the Society of Surfer Teachers—especially since he'd founded the club. Tucking the board under his arm, he headed for the door.

Debbie followed him. She waved good-bye, adding one last observation. "I just *love* that we all shared!"

Pim groaned in frustration. Alone in the office, she paced back and forth. "Everyone hates something," she muttered to herself, "even Berwick. Now I'm going to find out what that thing is. And when I do, I'll expose her for the fraud she really is!"

"I'm not a fraud," Debbie replied, suddenly

appearing at Pim's side. Pim nearly jumped through the ceiling.

"I'm a Capricorn," Debbie added cheerfully. "What's your sign?"

CHAPTER TWO

After school that day, Phil came home to find his mother in the backyard surrounded by pitchers of milk. Mrs. Diffy had lined the containers up all over the Diffys' outdoor furniture.

"Mmmm, butter," Mrs. Diffy sang as she pumped the handle of an old-fashioned wooden churn. "The everlasting delight of the gourmand! The faithful ally of the culinary art! Toast's best buddy!"

Phil scratched his head. Okay, he thought, either my mom's forgotten that you can buy butter at the grocery store in this time period, or she's trying one of those weird workout fads they're always peddling on twenty-first-century TV.

"Uh, Mom?" he called. "Can I talk to you for a sec?"

"Sure!" she exclaimed as she continued to work the churn. She noticed Phil staring at her eighteenth-century outfit. She wore an old-fashioned calico dress that reached almost to the ground, with a long, white apron tied over it. A white bonnet covered her short brown hair.

"I'm just reliving *la vida* time travel," she explained.

Oh, thought Phil, now I get it. Mom misses our old time-traveling life.

"Remember how much fun we had, Phil?" Mrs. Diffy continued. "Your dad popped a wheelie in that buggy cart, and Pim got bitten by the duck." Phil's mother paused for a second to concentrate on her churning. Up and down. Up and down. "Making butter is harder than it looks. Oh, man, my arms are cramping up."

"Sounds like you took a *churn* for the worst," Phil joked.

"Come on," she said, waving him to the picnic table on the lawn. "I could use a break." As they sat down, Mrs. Diffy poured her son a big glass of milk. "What's on your mind?" she asked, handing him the glass.

Phil cautiously sniffed the milk, making sure it hadn't been turned into *butter*milk yet. When he was satisfied, he took a sip. Then he explained what had happened after cheerleading tryouts. "I just don't get why Keely would lie to her mom like that."

"Oh, Phil, mothers and daughters have very complicated relationships. I know from personal experience." She sighed, thinking of Pim. And then, of course, there was her own mother—

"You and Grandma?" asked Phil.

Mrs. Diffy nodded. She told Phil that she could still recall the day she'd brought Phil's father home to meet her mother. In her younger years, Mrs. Diffy had been into synth-fur fashions and she'd worn her favorite pink vest for the occasion. Her hair had been much longer then, too.

"Mom, I know you have expectations," Mrs. Diffy had told her mother. "But I don't want to marry an astro-surgeon," she'd declared. "I'm in love with Lloyd, and he's a great guy."

Phil's father had worn his hair much longer then, too. "Yeah! Woo-hoo!" he'd exclaimed as he moonwalked into the room. "I love your daughter! I love her!" He tossed his long hair over his shoulder and finished his declaration with: "You got any food?"

Phil sighed after hearing this story. "I don't know," he mumbled. He didn't see how his mother's little flashback—er, flash *forward*—was going to help him now. Then again, he told himself, figuring out Keely's motives didn't exactly take a degree in trans-alien psychology. "I guess she just wants to make her mom happy."

"Yeah," said Mrs. Diffy. "But ultimately it won't, honey. Keely's got to tell her mother the truth sooner or later. And I know from personal experience, *sooner* is better."

Phil nodded. His mother was right. He had to convince Keely to come clean. "Thanks, Mom."

The next day, Phil persuaded Keely that honesty was the best policy—in any century. So after school, the two of them caught a bus over to Mrs. Teslow's real estate office.

When they reached the doorway, they hesitated. She was on the phone with one of her clients. And it didn't sound like it was going too well.

"It's a four-bedroom, two-bath *charmer*," Keely's mother cooed to the client on the other end of the phone line. But from the look on Mrs. Teslow's face, it seemed as if the client didn't believe her.

"Because I *say* it's a charmer," Mrs. Teslow

insisted into the phone. Phil heard some grumbles come through the receiver. "You know what?" replied Mrs. Teslow. "You're *not* a charmer."

Keely tensed and whispered to Phil, "She's busy. Maybe we should go."

Phil took hold of Keely's elbow to keep her from bolting. "No, you can do this."

Mrs. Teslow hung up the phone and finally noticed who was standing in her doorway. "Oh, what a surprise!" she cried, leaping to her feet. "What are you two doing here?"

Keely gulped as she crossed the room. "Just in the neighborhood. Thought we could talk."

"Of course," said Mrs. Teslow. "Sit. Sit. Please, sit!" She pointed to the two chairs in front of her desk. "Hey, would you like some water?" she asked.

Before Phil or Keely could answer, Mrs. Teslow opened a drawer in her desk and slapped a bottle of water on her desk.

"How about a promotional coffee mug? A

hat? Or some tube socks?" She threw freebie after freebie at Phil.

He juggled each one as they came flying at him. "Thanks."

Finally, Mrs. Teslow turned to Keely. "So, butternut, what did you want to talk about?"

Keely leaned forward in her chair. "Uh, well, it's about being a cheerleader," she began. "There can be a lot of pressure put on you—"

"Jelly bean," Keely's mom interrupted, "listen, I know right where this is going."

"You do?" asked Keely, hopefully.

Mrs. Teslow nodded compassionately. "When I was a cheerleader, I had to come up with new cheers all the time. It can be a lot of pressure on a person. So let me show you a little trade secret."

Keely's mom jumped up from her chair and crossed to a shrine in the corner of her office dedicated to her former cheerleading days. There was a collection of framed photos of her old cheerleading squad, her old cheerleading megaphone, spirit stick, and pom-poms. Keely's mom grabbed the pom-poms and stood in the "ready" position.

"Don't just go with the typical 'Rebound that basketball, rebound!'" she advised, shaking her pom-poms this way and that. "Change it up. Have fun. Be creative. '*Alley-oop* that basketball, alley-oop!' See what I did there? I just changed the word."

Phil tried not to cough from the dust that flew off the pom-poms. Keely shook her head in frustration. "Mom, Mom—"

"I know, I know," Mrs. Teslow replied, putting back the pom-poms and sitting down again. "I'm sorry. I'm getting a little carried away."

Suddenly, the intercom buzzed. "Mrs. Teslow," called the secretary's voice, "Mr. Phipps is on line two."

Mrs. Teslow pressed a button on her phone. "Put it through to voice mail, please."

Before Keely's mom could turn the speaker

down, her recorded greeting sang out, *"Duplex, condo, fixer-upper . . . Go with Teslow, close by supper!"* She grinned at Phil and Keely. "That's the new one," she informed them proudly.

Whoa, thought Phil, this woman is obsessed with cheerleading!

"Hello," said the caller on the voice mail. "Mrs. Teslow, this is Mr. Phipps. I really need to talk to you. . . ."

With a sigh, Keely's mom turned down the volume. "After I retire from real estate and you move out of the house," she told her daughter, "cheerleading will be the single most precious thing that gets me through the day."

Phil shuddered. "You're kidding."

"No," said Keely and her mom in unison.

Keely quietly sighed. What Phil didn't know was that his best friend's mother, aunt, and grandmother had all been cheerleaders. They had stacks of scrapbooks and photo albums to relive their memories of every game they'd ever attended. They had season tickets to three college teams—just to watch the spirit squads on the sidelines. And every year, when ESPN covered the National Cheerleading Competition, her mother threw a blowout reunion party for her old squad.

Mrs. Teslow leaned forward in her chair. "Well, now, is there anything else you wanted to talk about?"

"No," Phil said quickly. "No. Unless Keely has something."

"No," Keely agreed. *Good*, she thought. Now that Phil understands what I'm up against, I can keep living my cheerleading lie—and my mom *never* has to know.

"Guess what!" her mom cried. "I have Thursday afternoon off, so I can come and watch you cheer!"

Keely and Phil froze in their seats.

"What's the matter?" asked Mrs. Teslow.

"Nothing," Phil replied. "Nothing's the matter." And it was true—because a brilliant idea had just occurred to him. He jumped up from his seat. "Mrs. Teslow, I *promise you* this Thursday will be one of the *proudest* moments of your life."

Keely's mom melted into a puddle of parental mush. "Thank you," she said with tears in her eyes. Then she came around her desk and opened her arms to her daughter. "Come here, sweetie."

As Keely was pulled into a smothering hug, she shot Phil a look of pure panic. *Excuse me*, she wanted to scream, if I didn't make the team—*how* is my mother going to watch me cheer on Thursday?

But Phil wasn't worried. He already had the problem solved.

CHAPTER THREE

The next afternoon, Keely met up with Phil in a small park across from their school. "So we're actually going to cheer at a real football game?" she asked him excitedly.

"Not football," he told her. He'd already changed into a cheerleading outfit—a blue-and-white sweater with a big *W* embroidered on it and matching track pants.

"Oh, wrestling?" Keely guessed, examining the two girls' uniforms he had brought for her.

"No," Phil replied.

"Cross-country?" Keely asked hopefully.

"Nope," said Phil. "Billiards!"

Keely frowned. "Cheerleaders at a *billiards* match?"

Phil nodded. "Yeah."

Keely scratched her head. "I didn't even know Wells had a team."

"Exactly," said Phil. "See, the spirit squad has assigned a few of its members to every single sporting event at the school. That way, they can spread the spirit around a bit."

"Really?" Keely asked.

"No," admitted Phil. "But that's what you're going to tell your mom."

The whole thing had been pretty easy for Phil to arrange. Earlier that day, he had borrowed three cheerleading uniforms from a school storage closet. Then he scanned the activities bulletin board for events taking place the next day. He'd picked a game where no real cheerleaders were likely to show. Finally, he made two phone calls, one of them to Keely.

Wow, Phil. I love it," said Keely with relief. '*She's* gonna love it."

"Hey, if she wants to see you cheer, she's going to see you in all your peppy glory," Phil promised. Now all they had to do was put in a few hours of *unofficial* cheerleading practice.

Keely pointed to the hangers Phil was holding. "So, who's that other uniform for?"

"Hey, guys!" Keely's friend Tia cried as she raced up to them. She was dressed in a metallic skirt and blouse and matching gold earrings, necklace, and headband. "Did you get the call for this Santana video, too?" she asked.

Phil exchanged a sheepish look with Keely.

Tia saw it and her eyes narrowed on Phil. "That was *you* on the phone, wasn't it?"

"No!" he lied. "But now that you're here, Keely has a favor to ask you."

Tia shrugged. "You name it," she told her best friend. She pointed to the hangers in Phil's hand. "Just as long as I don't have to get into one of those cheerleading uniforms."

Keely bit her lip. Phil held out one of the hangers.

Tia raised an eyebrow. So, okay, she told herself, cheerleading isn't exactly a rock video. But maybe I can still show off some of my dance moves.

With another shrug, Tia took the uniform. "I am so easy," she said with a sigh. She held the sweater up to her gold necklaces. "And you *know* this girl's gonna accessorize."

Not far away in the same park, Pim was also engaged in an *unofficial* after-school activity—spying on Debbie Berwick. From her post halfway up a tree, Pim could see that Debbie was playing chess with an elderly woman. Probably one of her annoying help-the-elderly volunteer projects, Pim grumbled to herself.

"Knight to rook three," Debbie said, nodding. "I *love* that move, Reba."

The elderly woman smiled and nodded her head.

"I give up," muttered Pim. "She loves everything. Maybe it *is* possible to love all things. . . ." Pim considered this. Maybe she could try it herself. At that moment, a bright butterfly flew by. "Stupid butterfly!" Pim spat, waving the annoying insect away.

Just then, Pim noticed Reba offering Debbie a fresh scone. "Thank you," said Debbie. But as she took a closer look at the pastry, Debbie scowled. Up in the tree, Pim couldn't believe her eyes. Debbie actually *scowled*!

"Uh . . . no, thank you, Reba," Debbie said, handing back the pastry. "I love scones, just not *this* kind."

Pim's eyes brightened. "Hel-lo," she murmured. She pulled her father's Scanalyzer out of her pocket. "Let's see what's in that baby." Pim pressed a button on the device and the Scanalyzer sent a rebounding laser into the scone. What came back was the following data: *flour, sugar, milk, eggs . . .*

Pim shook her head. She didn't think

any of those ingredients were the problem.

Then the Scanalyzer listed one last ingredient: *raisins*.

A sly smile spread across Pim's face. "Well, well, well," she murmured. "Debbie don't do raisins."

The next afternoon, H.G. Wells's billiards team was fired up to win.

"Next up, the featherweight division—Seth Wosmer against Lefty Johnson," a cultured British voice softly announced over the Billiards Room loudspeaker.

In a corner of the room, Tia pushed up the sleeve of her long, red raincoat and glanced at her watch. "It's four o'clock," she told Phil and Keely, who were also wearing raincoats. "She's not here. Hey, maybe we're off the hook."

Keely nodded. "Maybe she got a traffic ticket. And because the officer was making her late, she got sassy with him. Then he put her in handcuffs and threw her in jail!" she suggested hopefully.

Just then, Mrs. Teslow pushed open the Billiards Room door.

"Guess she busted out," observed Tia. She, Keely, and Phil hurriedly threw off their raincoats. Underneath, they were wearing the borrowed cheerleading uniforms.

Mrs. Teslow rushed over to hug Keely. "Oh, sweetie, you look terrific!" she cried. Then she noticed Phil and Tia. "Hey, I didn't know you guys were on the squad."

Tia grinned. "*Totally*, Mrs. T," she said in a superbubbly voice.

Phil and Keely winced. Tia had never uttered a superbubbly "totally" in her life.

"What?" Tia replied defensively. "Cheerleaders don't say '*totally*' anymore?"

Mrs. Teslow looked around the Billiards Room. A small group of spectators sat quietly on low bleachers. Two players dressed in slacks, vests, and bow ties stood in front of a pool table, chalking up their cue sticks.

"So," said Keely's mom, a little confused.

"What happened to football? What happened to basketball? Now you're cheering pocket pool?"

"This has become a major sport, Mrs. T," Phil said, trying to sound convincing. "Very classy."

Tia nodded. "It's way bigger than tetherball."

Just then, the crowd broke out in polite applause. "And that knots up the match," the announcer softly declared. "Three games, Franklin—three games, Wells."

Mrs. Teslow clapped her hands with glee. "Oooh, crunch time!" she said before racing off to find a seat. It wasn't hard. The bleachers weren't exactly full.

"Come on, guys," Phil told his squad.

"Next up," murmured the British announcer, "Seth Wosmer to break."

A hush fell over the crowd as Seth squeaked the blue square of chalk back and forth on the tip of his cue stick. After a few seconds, however, he realized he'd been chalking his thumb instead. *Darn!* Seth thought. He quickly licked the chalk off, then grimaced. Pool chalk tasted *awful*!

Finally, Seth bent over the billiards table. The crowd quieted even more. Seth lined up the cue ball. He took a deep breath, pulled back his stick, and—

"Break shot!" Phil yelled through a megaphone. "Hey!" He clapped his hands. "It's time to break!"

"Big break!" Keely and Tia joined in, shaking their pom-poms. *Clap, clap.* "Big break!"

"Go!" Mrs. Teslow cheered from the audience. "Go, Seth!"

Seth shuddered and looked up. *Yikes!* he thought. Since when do we have cheerleaders at billiards matches? I sure didn't get *that* memo.

With another deep breath, Seth tried to recover his focus. He pulled back his stick and sent the white cue ball rolling. It struck the triangle of colorful balls at the other end of the table, scattering them. The crowd politely applauded.

Seth smiled, then bent over the table to line up a new shot. He was just about to make it when Phil shouted, "Roll call!"

Tia jumped up wearing a round, white helmet. "I'm cue ball," she chanted. "Don't knock me in."

"I'm cue stick," called Keely, spreading her arms wide. "I'm long and thin."

"I'm shooter," cried Phil, pushing Keely's arm into Tia's head. "I aim to win."

Seth shook his head at the ridiculous cheer. *Oh, man*, he thought, this is going to be one *long* match!

CHAPTER FOUR

"You wanted to see me, Mr. Hackett?" Debbie Berwick asked. She'd just found a note in her locker, asking her to stop by the counselor's office as soon as her last class was over.

The tall chair behind the counselor's desk slowly spun around. But Mr. Hackett wasn't in it.

"Pim!" Debbie cried in surprise.

"Mr. Hackett is away on school business," Pim purred. She folded her hands on the desktop. "Won't be back for some time."

Debbie frowned at Pim's outfit. Pim was

wearing a purple T-shirt that read MMMM, I LOVE RAISINS! and dangly earrings that looked like two tiny boxes of raisins.

"What's going on here?" Debbie demanded.

"Oh, I just dropped by to suggest a school field trip," Pim said, holding up a brochure, "to the *raisin* factory."

Debbie began to sweat. "Oh, um . . . th-that would be *f-fun*," she stammered.

"Would it?" asked Pim. "Because at the end of the factory tour, each student gets a complimentary box of . . . *raisins!*"

Debbie's eyes widened in horror as Pim pulled out an enormous box of raisins. She shook the box, and Debbie shuddered.

"Admit it, Berwick," said Pim, stepping around the desk. "You *hate* raisins."

"No, no . . . I don't . . ." Debbie protested, nervously backing up as Pim moved closer.

"So tiny and wrinkly." Pim pulled one out and waved it under Debbie's nose. "Some say they're nature's candy."

"Okay, fine!" Debbie cried, batting away the little dried fruit. "I hate raisins!" she confessed. Then she turned and ran down the hall, screaming, "I hate 'em! I hate 'em! I hate 'em!"

Pim watched her go. "Have I gone too far?" she wondered. For the first time in her life, Pim actually felt a twinge of something. Could it be my conscience? she wondered.

A second later, Pim burst out laughing. "Yeah, right!"

Meanwhile, in the H.G. Wells Billiards Room, the Phil Diffy cheer squad was still going strong. Unfortunately, they hadn't practiced enough to make every cheer perfect.

"What's the spin that Seth has got?" Phil shouted, jumping up and down.

"It's the spin that you have not," cried Keely and Tia, shaking their pom-poms.

"It's English!" cried Phil. "It's English!"

Just then, Keely's pom-pom accidentally slammed into Phil's stomach. *Ooof!* "Who's the team that's best in pool?" Phil chanted, coughing from the gut punch.

"It's the team that's from our school!" yelled Keely and Tia.

"It's Wells!" cheered Phil.

"No, duh?" cried Keely and Tia.

"It's Wells!" repeated Phil.

"No, duh?" echoed Keely and Tia.

In the half-empty bleachers, Mrs. Teslow glowed with pride. Even though Keely and Tia kept running into each other and Phil's timing was a *tad* off, she couldn't stop smiling. She tapped the shoulder of the man in front of her. "That's my daughter!" she told him.

"So, grab your cue and head on home!" shouted Phil.

"It's English time, so cheerio!" cried Keely and Tia. "Woo-hoo!"

After the unofficial cheerleaders sat down on the sidelines, Seth approached the pool table. His next shot could win the game—and the tournament.

"This is a nearly impossible bank shot for Wosmer," the announcer softly declared. As Seth quietly lined up the shot, the announcer suddenly decided to spice up his own act. "Seth's a ninth grader who, when he's not playing billiards, enjoys cable television and quiet dinners in his room."

At the billiards table, Seth rolled his eyes. *Great*, he thought. First I get rattled by shouting cheerleaders, and now the announcer treats me like a game show contestant!

Tension mounted as Seth pulled back his cue stick. The spectators fell into a stony silence. Suddenly, Mrs. Teslow got a little carried away. "Take 'em down, Seth!" she roared, jumping to her feet. "Take that turkey down!"

Phil could hardly keep from laughing at Mrs. Teslow's enthusiasm. "Look at her," he whispered to Keely sitting next to him. "This is like her dream come true."

Keely sighed. "Yeah, it is," she said sadly.

"What's the matter?" he asked. Keely was

supposed to be happy about this. But she suddenly looked miserable.

"Phil, it's *her* dream, not mine," Keely replied, realizing it for the first time. She stood up and began to pace. "My entire life, my mom has told me how great cheerleading would be." She walked to the billiards table and absently picked up the cue ball. "Mom was a cheerleader. Grandma Hayes was a cheerleader. Uncle Bruce wasn't a cheerleader, but he's real bubbly." She tossed the ball up and down while she thought. "But now I realize I don't want to be one."

"You should tell your mom that," Phil advised.

Keely nodded. She knew Phil was right.

Mrs. Teslow could see something was wrong, mainly because Keely hadn't even noticed she'd stopped the pool game dead. The players, the spectators, the announcer—*everyone* was waiting for her to return the white cue ball to the table. Mrs. Teslow climbed down from the bleachers and hurried over to her daughter.

"Mom," Keely said, facing her, "I'm really not a cheerleader. It's true. I'm sorry."

Mrs. Teslow's face fell. But then she seemed to realize it was okay. With a sad smile, she pulled Keely into a forgiving hug.

Just then, the announcer's soft voice came over the loudspeaker. "Will all mother/daughter conflicts please move to the parking lot? We've got a *game* here."

Keely suddenly realized she was holding the white cue ball. Seth held out his hand, and she tossed it to him. Then mother and daughter headed for the door.

Seth quickly lined up his shot again . . . and knocked the ball right into the pocket! He'd won the game *and* the tournament for H.G. Wells!

"Oh!" he cried, pumping his fist in the air. "I win! Sweet victory!" He looked around for the cheerleaders to join him. But Keely had left with her mother—and Phil was following them out the door. The only one left was Tia.

She rolled her eyes. Her *unofficial* cheerleading days were *officially* over.

"Wosmer," Tia said, "turn it down a notch."

CHAPTER FIVE

In the hall outside the Billiards Room, Tia ran up to join Phil and Keely. Phil was in the middle of explaining everything to Keely's mother.

"I'm sorry," he said. "It was a stupid plan, anyway. I mean, what were we going to do—become a roving band of cheer-bandits? I'm sorry, Mrs. Teslow."

Keely's mother smiled. "Phil, relax. It's fine," she said. Then she turned to Keely and grasped her shoulders. "Nugget, listen to me. You're my *person*, my most important person. And when you're being honest with yourself, like you were today, then you're being honest with me. Do you see how that works?"

Keely sighed with relief. "Wow, I feel like two huge cinder-block pom-poms have been lifted from my shoulders." She smiled. "Thank you, Mom."

"Oh, sweetie!" Mrs. Teslow cried and pulled her daughter into a hug. Then she noticed Phil and Tia. "Come on, you kids!" cried Mrs. Teslow, opening her arms wider. "You get in on this hug, too!"

After the group hug was over, Tia wiped away a tear. "This whole experience has definitely inspired me," she declared.

Phil was shocked. "You really want to become a cheerleader?"

"No," she said. "I've decided I'm going to tell my mom and dad about my *piercing*!"

For a few seconds, Phil, Keely, and Mrs. Teslow were dumbfounded. Then Keely's mother raised an eyebrow. "Good luck with that," she said flatly.

"Uh . . . that's . . . great," said Keely with an awkward thumbs-up.

Tia grinned and shook her pom-poms all the way back to the girls' locker room.

After the raisin assault in the counselor's office, Pim caught up with Debbie in the park across the street from their school.

"Debbie, do you realize everything you say is so . . . *happy*?" she asked.

Debbie stopped walking and shrugged. "What's wrong with being happy?"

Pim sighed. "Here's everyone else's happy," she said, holding her hand at waist level. "And here's *your* happy." She lifted her hand as high as it could go. "I can't even *reach* your happy. It's, like, fifty-foot-tall happy."

Debbie didn't see what was so bad about that. "Do you just like making fun of me?" she asked.

"No," said Pim sincerely. "I'm just trying to . . . you know, what's that thing nice people do after they do something bad? Um . . ."

"Apologize?" Debbie realized. "Oh, Pim, you're apologizing to me?"

Pim shrugged. "I don't know. I've never done it before."

"Ohmigosh, Pim! Here, let me help you." She reached out and took Pim's hand in hers. "Just repeat after me. 'Debbie, I'm sorry for hurting your feelings, because I know you're as fragile as a snowflake—'"

Pim shuddered. "I can't do this."

Debbie frowned. She let go of Pim's hand, then turned and began to walk away.

"Wait!" called Pim. She rushed up to Debbie again. "I want you to have this." Pim held up a plastic handle. A metal wire stuck out from each end. "It's a bucket handle," she explained. "It was on the ground. I thought it was cool looking, so I picked it up. Here."

Debbie took the bucket handle and studied it. The thing was totally useless, but it was a *gift*. An *apology* gift, she realized.

"Oh, Pim!" Debbie cried, overcome with emotion.

Pim tensed. *Uh-oh*, she thought, here it comes—the enthusiasm freight train.

"Oh! Maybe we should start a bucket-handles collection together!" Debbie exclaimed, jumping up and down. "I'll call you! Or better yet, we'll get walkie-talkies and we'll leave them on all night. This is going to be so much fun!"

Pim shook her head. *Yikes*, she thought as Debbie gave her a great, big hug. What was I *thinking*?

Later that afternoon, Pim hurried home. She finally understood why it could be good to be like Debbie. Now, Pim thought, I want to make the most of it.

She found her mother sitting on a lawn chair in the backyard. Mrs. Diffy's upper body was as stiff as a stone statue. She had been churning butter so long, she could no longer move her neck, shoulders, or arms.

Pim immediately went into mother's-little-helper mode. She made some toast and buttered it with all the fresh butter she could scoop from the churn, which wasn't much. Then she sat down in the lawn chair next to her mother's.

"I relish these quiet moments with you, Pim," said Mrs. Diffy. "I'd hug you if my arms weren't so cramped up from churning."

"Don't worry, Mom," said Pim. "Who could have imagined that twenty-one quarts of milk could only produce *one* measly pat of butter?" She smiled sweetly. "But yes, just us girls and some fresh buttered toast." She delicately lifted the buttered toast to her mother's mouth, careful to keep the butter from smearing on her face.

"Mmmm, mmmm!" Mrs. Diffy exclaimed after tasting it. "That's some good butter!"

Pim took a nibble. "Mmmm," she said, forcing a great big smile. Then she got down to business. "Since we're both happy as *kittens prancing in sunbeams*," she began, doing her best to channel Debbie Berwick, "can I get a bigger allowance?"

"No, sorry, sweetie," said Mrs. Diffy.

"But, Mom—" Pim protested.

"Mmmm, mmmm, that's some good butter," Mrs. Diffy interrupted, pointedly changing the subject.

With a sigh of frustration, Pim fed her mother more of the buttered toast—only this time she wasn't so careful.

"Mmmm," said her mother again as she chewed and swallowed.

Pim grinned. Oh, well, she thought. At least I know what makes me happy—getting even.

"Pim, is there something on my nose?" Mrs. Diffy asked.

Pim stared at the shiny spot of yellow butter on the tip of her mom's nose. "No, Mother," she said with a diabolical little smile. "You're golden."

CHECK OUT THE NEXT
PHIL OF THE FUTURE STORY!

Blast from the Past

Adapted by N.B. Grace

Based on the television series, "Phil of the Future", created by Douglas Tuber & Tim Maile

Based on the episode written by Dan Fybel & Rich Rinaldi

It was a dark and peaceful night. A soft breeze blew through the trees. Moonlight glimmered on the lawn. Mr. and Mrs. Diffy were fast asleep in their comfortable bed on the second floor of their lovely home. Everything was just as it should be—until the loud crash of breaking glass sounded from downstairs.

Mr. Diffy shook his wife awake. "Honey, wake up!" he said urgently. "I think I heard something."

Mrs. Diffy awoke immediately and sat straight up in bed. "What was it?" she asked as she jumped up and pulled on her robe, ready to do battle.

"Go down and check it out," Mr. Diffy suggested. "I'll hang back and guard the bed." His wife looked at him in disbelief. She was supposed to face an intruder all by herself, and he was going to "guard the bed"? Before she could protest, he added, "Can you bring me back a snack?"

"A snack?" Mrs. Diffy couldn't believe her ears. Burglars could be rampaging through their home, and her husband was thinking about having a bite to eat!

Mr. Diffy smiled at her. "Yeah, anything. Just surprise me."

In one swift movement, she snatched the comforter away and pulled him off the bed. "Surprise!" she yelled.

Her husband yelped in shock.

"You're coming with me," Mrs. Diffy said firmly.

They crept downstairs to find that Phil and Pim were already there. They had also been awakened by the crash. Now the family looked around the kitchen, noting the signs that showed a mysterious intruder had been there.

Mrs. Diffy held up a pan which, until a short time ago, had been filled with her delicious lasagna, already cooked for tomorrow night's family dinner. Now just a few scraps of food were left inside.

"Well, looks like *something* really enjoyed my lasagna," she said.

Pim held up an oven mitt with a huge

bite taken out of it. "Don't flatter yourself, Mom," she said. "It also enjoyed your oven mitt."

"Maybe we have mice," Phil suggested. Mice wouldn't be so bad. Mice could be dealt with. Although, he thought, that bite looked awfully big for a mouse.

His mother nodded and turned to his father. "Honey, looks like we need an exterminator," she said.

"Nonsense," Mr. Diffy said with his usual confidence as he took a plate of sandwiches from the refrigerator. "I can handle whatever's crawling around this house. Tomorrow morning, I'll go down to the hardware store and get some of that sticky paper."

Mr. Diffy's eyes gleamed as he looked at the two sandwiches, piled high with sliced turkey, cheese, lettuce, and tomatoes—not to mention that special gourmet mayo! Yum. "But right now, I want to slam down one of these bad boys for a little late-night pick-me-up."

Behind them, unseen by anyone in the Diffy family, the cupboard door under the sink slowly opened, revealing a caveman crouching under the pipes. His hair was long and matted, and he wore a tunic and boots made of fur. A leather necklace strung with several large pointed teeth hung around his neck.

Unaware that their nighttime visitor was still in the room, Phil eyed the other sandwich. "Leave the other one out, too, Dad," he said. "I could go for a little nosh myself."

"Good call, son." Mr. Diffy laughed. "The po'boy sandwich is one of the world's great discoveries."

Sniff, sniff. The caveman could smell the sandwiches from across the room. And he had to agree with Mr. Diffy and Phil—they smelled absolutely *delicious*. He crept out of the cupboard and began cautiously moving across the kitchen.

Pim somehow sensed that something was . . . different. She quickly turned to look over her shoulder, but the caveman ducked behind the kitchen island even more quickly. Hmm, Pim thought, as she looked around the kitchen, which appeared to be completely normal. My nerves must be on edge with all this late-night excitement.

She turned back to see her father unwrapping the sandwiches with anticipation. Somehow, being awakened in the middle of the night and discovering signs of a mysterious intruder made a person very, very hungry. No one noticed the caveman as he sneaked out of the kitchen.

"Now, that's what I call a midnight snack," Mr. Diffy said.

Pim's and Phil's eyes lit up.

"Yeah, sure is," Phil said.

"Thanks, Dad," Pim said.

They each grabbed a sandwich and dashed out of the kitchen to enjoy their snack in their rooms.

"Oh . . ." Mrs. Diffy sighed as she and her

husband watched the po'boys vanish along with their kids.

A few minutes later, sleepy and still a little hungry, Mr. and Mrs. Diffy got back into bed, ready for what was left of a good night's sleep.

Mrs. Diffy made a face as she smelled a frankly awful smell. She looked accusingly at her husband. "Uh . . . Lloyd! Awww . . ."

"I didn't do nothin'," he protested. He wrinkled his nose. He hadn't done anything, but *something* smelled pretty rank.

Then he felt something warm push against his feet and he laughed. "Honey, I'll take a rain check on the footsies, okay?"

His wife looked at him with dawning horror. "That's not my foot. . . ." she said slowly.

She sat up, and they stared at each other. If it wasn't his wife's foot, Mr. Diffy thought, then what . . . ?

With one motion, Mr. and Mrs. Diffy flipped back the comforter—and revealed the caveman at the foot of their bed!

Mr. and Mrs. Diffy screamed in shock.

The caveman screamed even louder in surprise.

Then they all screamed together, and the caveman jumped off the bed and ran out the door.

a COMEDY OF
PSYCHIC PrOPOrTIONS!
that's SO
raven
every DaY on
DISNEY CHANNEL!
DISNEY
CHANNEL
ORIGINAL
DISNEYCHANNEL.COM

Dragon Booster

THE NEW BOOK SERIES

COMING TO A STORE NEAR YOU

September 2005

VOLO
an imprint of
Hyperion Books
for Children

STOVE HAT

ALLIANCE
ATLANTIS

Betty and Veronica wear the latest fashions, know what's cool, and are always up for some fun. Now they are telling all to their fans! Full of humor and attitude, these books will show you how to deal with everything from school to boys—all from the perspective of two famous and fabulous best friends . . . and crush rivals!

Available wherever books are sold!

For more fun with Archie and the gang, log onto www.archiecomics.com.

HYPERION
BOOKS FOR CHILDREN
miramax books

TM & © 2005 Archie Comic Publications, Inc